D1710117

Women Who Built Our Scientific Foundations

Major Women in Science

Women Who Built Our Scientific Foundations

Kim Etingoff

Mason Crest

Mason Crest
450 Parkway Drive, Suite D
Broomall, Pennsylvania 19008
www.masoncrest.com

Printed and bound in the United States of America.

First printing
9 8 7 6 5 4 3 2 1

Series ISBN: 978-1-4222-2923-1
ISBN: 978-1-4222-2933-0
ebook ISBN: 978-1-4222-8902-0

The Library of Congress has cataloged the
        hardcopy format(s) as follows:

            Library of Congress Cataloging-in-Publication Data

Etingoff, Kim.
  Women who built our scientific foundations / Kim Etingoff.
      pages cm. – (Major women in science)
  Audience: Grade 7 to 8.
  Includes bibliographical references and index.
    ISBN 978-1-4222-2933-0 (hardcover) – ISBN 978-1-4222-8902-0 (ebook) –
ISBN 978-1-4222-2923-1 (series)
  1. Women scientists–Biography–Juvenile literature. 2. Science–Vocational guidance–
Juvenile literature. I. Title.
  Q141.E75 2014
  509.2'52–dc23
                                        2013011151

Produced by Vestal Creative Services.
www.vestalcreative.com

Contents

Introduction

Have you wondered about how the natural world works? Are you curious about how science could help sick people get better? Do you want to learn more about our planet and universe? Are you excited to use technology to learn and share ideas? Do you want to build something new?

Scientists, engineers, and doctors are among the many types of people who think deeply about science and nature, who often have new ideas on how to improve life in our world.

We live in a remarkable time in human history. The level of understanding and rate of progress in science and technology have never been greater. Major advances in these areas include the following:

- Computer scientists and engineers are building mobile and Internet technology to help people access and share information at incredible speeds.
- Biologists and chemists are creating medicines that can target and get rid of harmful cancer cells in the body.
- Engineers are guiding robots on Mars to explore the history of water on that planet.
- Physicists are using math and experiments to estimate the age of the universe to be greater than 13 billion years old.
- Scientists and engineers are building hybrid cars that can be better for our environment.

Scientists are interested in discovering and understanding key principles in nature, including biological, chemical, mathematical, and physical aspects of our world. Scientists observe, measure, and experiment in a systematic way in order to test and improve their understanding. Engineers focus on applying scientific knowledge and math to find creative solutions for technical problems and to develop real products for people to use. There are many types of engineering, including computer, electrical, mechanical, civil, chemical, and biomedical engineering. Some people have also found that studying science or engineering can help them succeed in other professions such as law, business, and medicine.

Both women and men can be successful in science and engineering. This book series highlights women leaders who have made significant contributions across many scientific fields, including chemistry, medicine, anthropology, engineering, and physics. Historically, women have faced barriers to training and building careers in science,

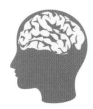

6

which makes some of these stories even more amazing. While not all barriers have been overcome, our society has made tremendous progress in educating and advancing women in science. Today, there are schools, organizations, and resources to enable women to pursue careers as scientists or engineers at the highest levels of achievement and leadership.

The goals of this series are to help you:

1. Learn about women scientists, engineers, doctors, and inventors who have made a major impact in science and our society
2. Understand different types of science and engineering
3. Explore science and math in school and real life

You can do a lot of things to learn more about science, math, and engineering. Explore topics in books or online, take a class at school, go to science camp, or do experiments at home. More important, talk to a real scientist! Call or e-mail your local college to find students and professors. They would love to meet with you. Ask your doctors about their education and training. Or you can check out these helpful resources:

- *Nova* has very cool videos about science, including profiles on real-life women scientists and engineers: www.pbs.org/wgbh/nova.
- *National Geographic* has excellent photos and stories to inspire people to care about the planet: science.nationalgeographic.com/science.
- Here are examples of online courses for students, of which many are free to use:
  1. Massachusetts Institute of Technology (MIT) OpenCourseWare highlights for high school: http://ocw.mit.edu/high-school
  2. Khan Academy tutorials and courses: www.khanacademy.org.
  3. Stanford University Online, featuring video courses and programs for middle and high school students: online.stanford.edu.

Other skills will become important as you get older. Build strong communication skills, such as asking questions and sharing your ideas in class. Ask for advice or help when needed from your teachers, mentors, tutors, or classmates. Be curious and resilient: learn from your successes and mistakes. The best scientists do.

Learning science and math is one of the most important things that you can do in school. Knowledge and experience in these areas will teach you how to think and how the world works and can provide you with many adventures and paths in life. I hope you will explore science—you could make a difference in this world.

Ann Lee-Karlon, PhD
President
Association for Women in Science
San Francisco, California

1

What Does It Take to Be a Scientist?

Scientists ask big questions about the world. They investigate new sources of energy. They have discovered the laws of physics. They create new drugs to cure illnesses. Scientists play large roles in our lives today, so it's no wonder many people **aspire** to be scientists someday.

Not long ago, though, science was only an option for men. Women had no place in science, and they were discouraged from pursuing it as a career. Thankfully, things have changed, and our society is now much more accepting of

School is a good place to explore science. Today's students may be tomorrow's scientists.

women who are scientists. More and more women are becoming chemists, medical doctors, **geologists**, and other kinds of scientist. Women scientists and female science students still face challenges, but they have made great strides in the past hundred years.

Today, there are millions of scientists today of both genders. The National Science Foundation reported the United States alone had more than 3.8 million scientists in 2010, people who chose to pursue science as a fulfilling and worthwhile career.

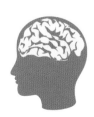

A Dream

We all have to take science classes in school. Students' first experiences in a science class might inspire a dream to become a scientist. For example, a student who finds high school biology fascinating might go on to become a biologist or a medical doctor. A student who likes earth science class might become a geologist, **hydrologist**, or **atmospheric scientist**.

Some children know they want to be scientists from a very young age. Many of those children have family members who are scientists. Maybe they visit their mom at a university physics lab, or they talk to their dad about what it's like to be a doctor. They are taught that science is important, and to them, it seems like a normal way to make a living.

Another reason some people become scientists is because they want to make the world a better place. There are lots of ways of improving lives, and science is one of them. Science has changed the world time and time again. Think about discoveries like penicillin and electricity! Can you imagine what the world would be like without them? Scientists change the world in real and measurable ways through their research and discoveries.

Not all scientists will come up with the discovery of the century, but all scientific research does help us understand our world a little more. Future scientists may build on that research to come with the discovery that does **revolutionize** how we live. One scientist may be driven by the need to advance knowledge about solar energy so that we can slow climate change. Another may spend her life researching a vaccination that could prevent a certain kind of cancer.

Getting an Education

Students who are serious about becoming scientists have to be **dedicated** to their dream. Their path is long and requires a lot of education. Some students spend nine years or more in science-focused school before they can be considered ready for a high-level job in their chosen field.

After graduating from high school, future scientists have to go to college. In college, they start to focus on what kind of science they would like to pursue. Colleges offer bachelor's degrees in natural sciences, which include biology,

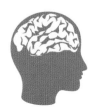

chemistry, physics, and earth science. A student might also major in a social science, such as psychology, **anthropology**, **economics**, or **political science**. An undergraduate degree usually takes four years. Students start with introductory classes, and then take coursework with a more specific focus in their final years of college. They might have opportunities to work in a professor's lab, become a **teaching assistant**, or maybe even help publish a paper.

After college, most people who are serious about becoming scientists must go on to get a more advanced degree. There are a few jobs for scientists with a bachelor's degree, but most positions require a master's degree or a PhD. Master's degrees take one to three years; PhDs require more time—five years or more. While getting a PhD, students take a few classes and then work in labs doing research in their chosen fields. PhD students focus on very specific scientific fields and start to become experts in them.

After receiving PhDs, some people still need to go through one more step before they become employed scientists. Many people with PhDs must get post-doctoral **fellowships**. They need a little more experience doing research, so they spend a few years continuing their research as post-doctoral fellows.

After all of that, the aspiring scientist finally can apply for jobs at universities doing research and teaching, in businesses, or for the government.

What Else Does It Take to Be a Scientist?

It takes more than just a good education to be a good scientist. People who want to do well at their jobs also need to have other qualities.

Scientists need to be patient and dedicated. First, it takes a long time to become a scientist. Students need patience while getting their education, and focus on the knowledge they are building while in school. Without patience, it's hard to stick with working toward a science degree for years. Scientists also need to be patient in the lab. Experiments may take a long time to perform, and may require observations over many months or years. Giving up or speeding up an experiment is not an option for scientists.

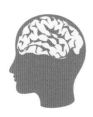

12 Scientific Foundations

People practicing science must also be detail-oriented. Every experiment is planned out exactly. Nothing can be overlooked or sloppy. Scientists also read lots of research papers before they design their own experiments. They have to pay attention to the details in those studies and remember them.

Scientists also need to be good at writing and communicating. The way that scientists tell the world about their work is through research papers. They must be able to write clearly and correctly. Scientists also give lectures in schools and at conferences, write research proposals to get money for their projects, and more. All those things depend on good writing and communication skills.

To Sum It All Up

A certain kind of people are attracted to science as a career. These people like to ask questions, and they have the curiosity and dedication to become scientists. Many of those scientists today are women, and even more women will become scientists in the future.

In the past, when being a woman scientist was a hard thing to achieve, a few passionate women broke the barriers and became scientists. These women laid the foundations on which other scientists would build in a wide range of scientific studies. And these women also laid foundations for other women who would follow in their footsteps to become scientists as well.

Words to Know

Aspire: to strive to achieve something.

Geologists: scientists who study the earth's physical structure and the processes that create that structure; geologists study subjects such as rocks, water, air, and glaciers.

Hydrologist: a scientist who studies the distribution and use of water on Earth.

Atmospheric scientist: a person who studies the layer of gases, called the atmosphere, surrounding the earth.

Revolutionize: to change a lot.

Dedicated: devoted to a cause or purpose; choosing to spend a lot of time reaching a particular goal.

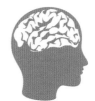

Anthropology: the study of human beings and their cultures, both in the past and in the present.

Economics: a social science dealing with the study of goods and services, along with their creation, distribution, and use.

Political science: a social science that focuses on the study of governments.

Teaching assistant: a person, usually an advanced student, who helps a professor teach a class, often by grading papers, leading discussions, and tutoring other students.

Fellowships: monetary awards given out to students or professionals to pursue a research project.

Find Out More

Karnes, Frances A. *Young Women of Achievement: A Resource for Girls in Science, Math, and Technology*. Amherst, N.Y.: Prometheus, 2002.

National Science Foundation: "Employment and Educational Characteristics of Scientists and Engineers"
www.nsf.gov/statistics/infbrief/nsf13311/start.cfm?org=NSF

Science Buddies: "Careers in Science"
www.sciencebuddies.org/science-fair-projects/science_careers.shtml

Wyatt, Valerie. *The Science Book for Girls and Other Intelligent Beings*. Toronto, Canada: Kids Can Press, 2008.

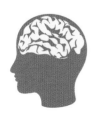

2

Long-Ago Women in Science

When did science start? Who were the first women scientists? No one really knows the answers to those questions—but people, including women, have been investigating the world around them for as long as human beings have existed.

Prehistoric Science

We don't really know a lot about what life was like for prehistoric people. Scientists can guess some things from looking at ancient **artifacts**, graves, and cave paintings, but many things are still a mystery to us. We know that prehistoric people understood something about medicine, since **archaeologists** have found **medicinal** plants and herbs with bodies that are thousands of years old.

Medicine and magic were very much connected in those days, though, and doctors were more like shamans—people who use magic and the spirit world to help cure diseases and predict the future.

We don't know a lot about the role women played in prehistoric societies either. Sometimes, the way archaeologists and historians interpret the evidence tells us more about what archeologists and historians believe themselves than what was really going on in people's lives thousands of years ago. Some believe that women were the leaders in prehistoric society, while others think they acted almost as servants. The truth is most likely somewhere in the middle.

In 2005, a group of archaeologists discovered a grave in northern Israel containing the skeleton of a woman who had lived around 12,000 years ago. The woman had been about forty-five years old when she died, and her back and hips were deformed so that she would have walked with a limp. Buried with her were parts of animals—like a cow's tail, an eagle's wing, the leg of a wild boar, and fifty tortoise shells—along with a human foot. The archaeologists who have been studying this gravesite think the woman was probably a shaman, a healer, making her one of the earliest women doctors we know about.

Science in Ancient Egypt

Medicine in ancient Egypt was a combination of science and magic. The Egyptians knew a little about how the body worked and what made people sick, but they believed evil spirits caused many sicknesses. Egyptian doctors—called *sunu*—treated some things with herbs and medicines. Other things, they treated by calling on the gods and asking them to drive out the evil spirits that were causing the illness.

Unlike most ancient societies, women in Egypt were often (although not always) treated equally with men. Women could own property, take men to court, and hold important positions. One woman, Merit Ptah, was an Egyptian doctor who lived nearly five thousand years ago. She is the first woman in history to be listed by name as a doctor.

We don't know very much about Merit Ptah, but her son, who was a High Priest, **memorialized** her on the wall of a tomb. Beside her picture, he wrote that

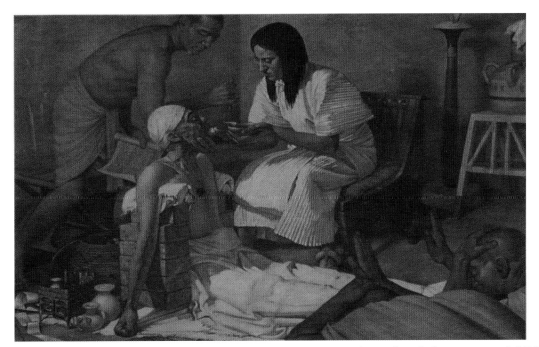

This painting captures a moment in the life of an Egyptian physician around 1500–1400 BCE. The artist included actual details recorded in ancient scrolls. The patient is supported by a "brick chair," and priests offer their prayers for healing

she was "the Chief Physician." This means that not only was she a doctor, but she was an important doctor.

Another important female doctor from ancient Egypt was Peseshet. She is described as having been the "female overseer of the women physicians." Some archaeologists think that she might have been in charge of the medical school at Sais, a school specifically for women. The women trained at Sais were a type of **midwife**. They had more training that the usual traditional midwives, but were considered less capable than doctors. They treated only women and were a kind of early **gynecologist** or **obstetrician**.

Ancient Greece

During the third or fourth century BCE, a woman in Athens, Greece, named Agnodice decided she wanted to become a doctor. She cut off her hair and disguised herself as a man in order to go to medical school. After she graduated, Agnodice wanted to treat female patients, but the women didn't accept her, because they thought she was a man. When they discovered she was a woman, she became very successful.

Long-Ago Women in Science 17

The male doctors were jealous of Agnodice's success and suspicious of her popularity with the female patients. When they discovered that Agnodice was a woman, they brought her to court to stop her from practicing medicine.

The wives of the city leaders scolded their husbands: "You are acting as our enemies, because Agnodice has brought us health and you are trying to stop her." Realizing their wives were right, the men changed the law to allow women to study medicine.

Most historians think Agnodice probably wasn't a real person, but midwives have been telling her story for hundreds of years to show why it's important that women be allowed to practice medicine.

Words to Know

Artifacts: things made by human beings, especially things that are historically important or interesting.

Archaeologists: scientists who study the people and cultures of the past by uncovering and looking at the things they left behind.

Medicinal: used as a medicine, to treat diseases or help with pain.

Memorialized: created something intended to keep a memory alive.

Midwife: a woman who helps women during childbirth.

Gynecologist: a doctor who focuses on women's health.

Obstetrician: a doctor who focuses on childbirth and on women's health related to childbirth.

Find Out More

History for Kids: "Ancient Greek Science"
www.historyforkids.org/learn/greeks/science/

Nutton, Vivian. *Ancient Medicine*. New York: Routledge, 2012.

Woods, Geraldine. *Science in Ancient Egypt*. Danbury, Conn.: Franklin Watts, 2008.

3

Emilie du Chatelet:
Scientific Genius of the 18th Century

Many female scientists did work that deserved to be famous, but because history did not record their names, their stories have been lost. Other women's names were recorded, but hardly anyone has heard of them. The physicist Emilie du Chatelet is one of them.

Emilie du Chatelet was born in 1706 in Paris. Her family was very wealthy, and she grew up in a large home with many servants. Her father was part of the French court. He could tell his only daughter was very intelligent, and so he set her up with teachers in languages, literature, math, science, and more. She did extremely well in math and science even at a young age, and she also became fluent in many languages.

Emilie was not only known for her brilliance. As a child (and in her adult life), she was known for speaking her mind and behaving unexpectedly. She cared more about books than clothes, and she loved to listen to astronomers who came to visit her father. This was not the way a young girl was supposed to behave back then. Her mother was horrified by her behavior, but her father didn't mind. He helped her make the most of her talents.

When she was eighteen, Emilie married the Marquis of Chastellet. He was a soldier and was often away on military business. They didn't spend much time together, and she was free to focus on her own interests. Even as a married woman and mother of three children, Emilie continued her studies in physical science and math, which was very unusual at the time. She was extremely smart and motivated, and was soon doing her own research.

She also hosted **salons** during these years. At each salon, she would invite great thinkers and scientists to talk about their thoughts and research. When she was in her twenties, she met Voltaire, a famous French thinker. They formed a bond and began investigating the world together.

Who Was Voltaire?

Voltaire is the pen name of François-Marie Arouet, a French writer and philosopher who lived during the eighteenth century. He is famous for his beliefs in basic freedoms, such as the freedom of religion and the freedom of expression. His ideas helped shape the American Revolution.

Together, Emilie and Voltaire set up a research lab in a French castle. Emilie focused on physics and math, and she published several scientific papers. Scientific visitors came to see the lab and stayed to discuss Emilie's most recent research.

For a while, she studied light and heat. She was interested in fire, and she published a paper titled "Essay on the Nature and Spread of Fire." Her studies were the first research into what we know today as **infrared radiation**, although she is not usually given credit as the scientist who discovered this kind of radiation.

$E = mc^2$

This equation means that energy (E) equals mass (m) times the square of the speed of light (c x c or c^2). Einstein's equation is important because it tells us that anything with mass has energy, and that we can change anything with mass into energy.

Emilie du Chatelet also contributed to the famous equation $E = mc^2$. Most people know that Albert Einstein proved that $E = mc^2$. However, his work was based on many scientists that came before him, and Emilie was one of them.

Sir Isaac Newton, another physicist, had thought a lot about energy. He thought that the energy of a moving object equaled the object's mass multiplied by its **velocity**. In other words, Newton thought E = mv. (Einstein's theory has to do with the velocity of light in particular, which he called "c"). Emilie had read Newton's theories. She disagreed with him, and she thought that his conclusions about energy were incorrect.

Voltaire, her partner, believed that Newton had been correct, though. That didn't stop Emilie from continuing to investigate. In the end, she concluded that Newton was wrong. She thought that the relationship between energy, mass, and velocity was actually $E = mv^2$, which was very close to what Einstein would prove centuries later. Scientists today recognize her as the first person to demonstrate this theory.

Emilie became very familiar with Isaac Newton's theories and work. During her later years, she started to translate his most famous book, the *Principia Mathematica*. The original was written in English, but she wanted French-speaking audiences to be able to read it as well. Besides translating the original, she also added her own notes and comments. She finished her translation the year she died, but it wasn't published until ten years later. It was very popular when it was finally published.

When Emilie was forty, she found out that she was pregnant. At that time, a pregnancy so late in life was very dangerous. Emilie herself believed her pregnancy was a death sentence, and so she prepared for the worst. She gave birth to a daughter in September 1749. Unfortunately, she had been right, and she died a week later. Her daughter died a little more than a year later.

Emilie du Chatelet's name isn't often mentioned in history books or science textbooks. However, more people are beginning to recognize her contributions to physics, as well as to the advancement of women in science. She laid important foundations that other scientists could build on.

Words to Know

Salons: regular gatherings of intellectual people.

Infrared radiation: Infrared radiation is part of the electromagnetic spectrum, which includes all the colors of light we can see with our eyes. Every kind of light is made up of waves, some of which are shorter and some of which are longer. Infrared radiation is light with long waves. Our eyes can't see infrared radiation, but we can feel it as heat.

Velocity: how fast an object is traveling in a certain direction.

Find Out More

Bodanis, David. *Passionate Minds: Emilie du Chatelet, Voltaire, and the Great Love Affair of the Enlightenment*. New York: Three Rivers Press, 2006.

The Human Touch of Chemistry: "Emilie du Chatelet"
humantouchofchemistry.com/emilie-du-chatelet.htm

Zinsser, Judith. *Emilie du Chatelet: Daring Genius of the Enlightenment*. New York: Penguin Books, 2006.

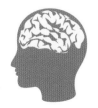

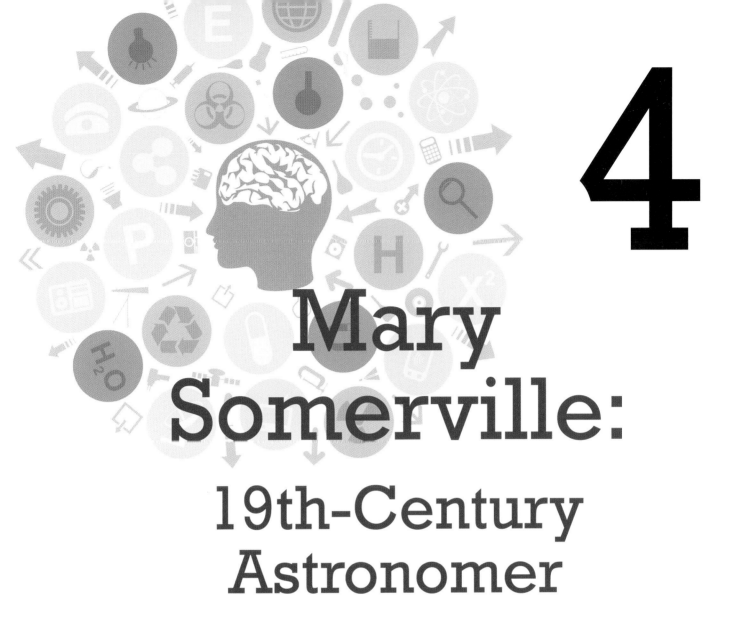

Mary Somerville:
19th-Century Astronomer

Even the most well-trained scientists can struggle with writing and communicating about science. One woman who was particularly good at making science understandable to students and scientists alike was Mary Somerville.

Mary Somerville was born Mary Fairfax on December 26, 1780, in Scotland. She grew up in Fife, Scotland, in a seaport town on the ocean. Her childhood was fairly normal for a young Scottish girl growing up in the late eighteenth century. Her father was an officer in the British Navy, and he was often not at home. Mary spent time at a boarding school for girls, but she did not receive much mathematical or scientific education. She only started studying arithmetic when she was thirteen. She spent most of her time exploring the seashore, and helping her mother around the house.

Mary wrote in her autobiography that she felt it was "unjust that women should have been given a desire for knowledge if it were wrong to acquire it." She described herself as being "intensely ambitious to excel in something, for I felt in my own breast that women were capable of taking a higher place in creation than that assigned to them in my early days, which was very low."

As a teenager, she discovered a math problem in a women's fashion magazine while she was at a tea party. She was intrigued, and convinced her brother's teacher to help her learn basic algebra. He gave her a copy of the famous mathematician Euclid's *Elements of Geometry*. Because Mary was a girl, her mother was upset that she was reading it. She tried to stop her daughter from reading any more about math.

Mary married her cousin Samuel Greig in 1804. She had two children with him. Her husband was not very supportive of her interest in math either, so she did not get very far with her studies during her marriage to him. Samuel died in 1807, though, leaving her with some inherited money and the freedom to keep studying math. Mary started collecting science, nature, and math books, and eventually, created a small library. Besides math, she liked to read about astronomy and the natural sciences.

In 1812, she married again. This time, her husband—Dr. William Somerville—supported her interests. They had several children together, but Mary still found time to study her books.

By 1825, Somerville felt confident enough to start experimenting herself. She had read a lot about scientific experiments, and she had some ideas of her own

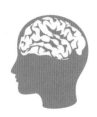

that she wanted to try out. Her first experiments had to do with magnets and led to a paper called "The Magnetic Properties of the Violet Rays of the Solar Spectrum." The Royal Society, a group of scientists in London, accepted her paper. It was only the second paper written by a woman the organization had ever accepted.

This paper was only the first of Mary's many scientific writings. She earned a reputation as a good scientific writer. She could write so that non-scientists could understand complicated subjects.

Her first famous work of scientific writing was a translation of the *Mecanique Celeste* (Celestial Mechanics) by Pierre-Simon Laplace, a French scientist. As soon as it was published, scientists adopted it as a **classic**. Her translation became a university textbook. Somerville had made hard-to-understand concepts easier to read about and comprehend.

She wrote many more books over the next few years. They included *On the Connexion of the Physical Sciences*, *Physical Geography*, and *Molecular and Microscopic Science*. They received a lot of praise, and were used in schools to teach young scientists. When she was eighty-nine, she published her last book *Molecular and Microscopic Science*.

Mary Somerville was one of the most successful female scientists in the early 1800s. The Royal Astronomical Society in England asked her to join their society because of her work. She was one of the first two women to join, a sign that she was well respected as a scientist despite her gender. The other woman who joined at around the same time was the astronomer Caroline Herschel.

The Royal Society

The Royal Society is probably the oldest group dedicated to science in the world. It was founded in 1660 in London, England, to promote scientific learning, and has been meeting ever since. The Royal Society is still in operation today, advising the British government and the United Nations, publishing papers, and funding research projects.

Mary spent her last years in Italy. She continued to be involved in scientific inquiry, and also put together an autobiography that was published after her death. She died at ninety-two. She had continued working on science and math problems until the day she died.

Words to Know

Classic: a book or other work considered to be excellent and has been or will be read or used for years to come.

Find Out More

Collective Biographies of Women: "Mary Somerville"
womensbios.lib.virginia.edu/featured?id=MARY_SOMERVILLE

Neeley, Kathryn A. *Mary Somerville: Science, Illumination, and the Female Mind.* New York: Cambridge University Press, 2001.

She Is an Astronomer: "Mary Somerville"
www.sheisanastronomer.org/index.php/history/mary-somerville

Who Was Caroline Herschel?

Caroline Herschel was a German-British astronomer who lived from 1750 to 1848. Though her childhood was unhappy and she wasn't given much of an education, she later went on to become the first woman to discover a comet. During her lifetime, she built telescopes, made astronomical calculations, discovered comets and nebulae, and created catalogues of stars. Her brother was fellow astronomer William Herschel. He taught her mathematics and helped her begin her studies in astronomy. Brother and sister worked together on many projects for the rest of their lives.

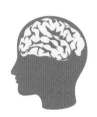

5

Florence Nightingale:
Creator of Modern Nursing

Almost everyone is familiar with the "Lady with the Lamp." The nickname is mostly a product of folklore and not exactly accurate, but there is no doubt that Florence Nightingale made a lasting contribution to the medical field.

Florence Nightingale was born in Florence, Italy, on May 12, 1820. Her parents, William and Fanny, named her after the city. Florence was born into a wealthy family. Her father was a well-connected British landowner, and he and his wife enjoyed a full social life. Florence and her sister, Parthenope (who was born in Naples, Italy, two years earlier, and given that city's ancient name), learned math, history, and languages from their father.

Florence not only changed medical care; she was also a gifted mathematician. She is considered to be a pioneer in the visual presentation of mathematical information, using charts and graphs that at the time had never or seldom been used (like the pie graph).

When it came time for Florence to decide how she would use that education and spend her time as an adult, Florence was torn. Part of her longed for a life like her parents'—marriage, children, and parties. But part of her wanted something more serious.

In 1837, Florence experienced what she believed was a religious calling (she continued to have such religious experiences throughout her life). Florence was certain she was meant to do more with her life than attend parties. She quickly found, however, that employment opportunities for women were rare. Women were meant to marry young and raise a family, not work outside the home.

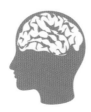

In 1844, Florence began to visit hospitals in and around London, searching for possible careers. The most obvious career was nursing, but it was not considered a desirable position—especially for someone from Florence's social circle. During that time, nursing was considered a profession that almost anyone could do; it required no education in the subject and little intelligence, and some people believed those who worked in nursing had low **morals**. Working conditions for nurses were poor and sometimes dangerous. This was especially true where the poor were treated, and that was the area that most interested Florence. Despite her family's strong objections—they thought nursing was no career for their daughter, who had had nothing but the best—Florence was sure this was the career to which God was calling her.

Florence spent the winter and spring of 1849 to 1850 in Egypt with family friends. During the trip from Paris to Egypt, she met two St. Vincent de Paul nuns. When they arrived in Alexandria, the sisters gave her a tour of their **convent**. Florence could immediately see the sisters were much more **disciplined** and organized than the nurses back in England.

In 1850, her parents gave her permission to spend a few months at the Institute of Protestant Deaconesses in Kaiserswerth, Germany. The institute had been founded in 1833 to care for the poor and had grown into a training school for women teachers and nurses. What she found there convinced Florence that it was possible to make nursing a respectable career for women.

In 1851, Florence studied at Kaiserswerth to become a sick nurse, as she called those who treated someone who was ill. (She called those who helped maintain health, health nurses.) When she returned home, she inspected hospitals in London, Edinburgh, and Dublin. In 1853, she accepted her first **administrative** position, superintendent of the Hospital for Invalid Gentlewomen.

In 1854, Florence organized a group of nurses to serve in the Crimean War. They were stationed at a British base hospital in Turkey. Already bad conditions rapidly worsened as increasing numbers of wounded were admitted to the hospital. Resources were inadequate, and what there were often did not go to those most in need. Florence and the other nurses worked in an area with contaminated water. To Florence, it seemed as though the British military treated their

injured soldiers as though they were disposable. Doctors did not take the nurses' input seriously.

Florence set out to change that. She had not brought the nurses all that way to be thrust aside. She convinced the doctors to accept her and the other nurses. She also helped financially. Through her efforts, a great deal of money was raised to purchase much-needed supplies.

After the end of the Crimean War in 1956, Florence returned to England. She was now legendary as the "Lady with the Lamp." In truth, Florence had not done much nursing in the wards during the war. Her real strength was in raising awareness and funds. She had influence in high circles—including royalty—and she was not afraid to use it to get what was needed to aid the sick and injured.

Through her experience in the Crimean War, Florence learned what had to be done to make hospitals run more smoothly and **efficiently**. She also became involved in **public health** issues. By 1858, Florence was recognized as an expert in water **sanitation** in India. She also worked to expand the use of irrigation as a way to combat the growing problem of famine.

In 1859, Florence supervised the founding of the Nightingale School, a training school for nurses, at London's St. Thomas's Hospital. Each year, twenty to thirty students learned about nursing through coursework as well as duties at the hospital.

Florence chose to devote herself to her work rather than to marry and have a family. Yet, she did not consider herself a **feminist**. She often commented that she thought the women of the day were lazy. Though a women's rights movement was growing in England, Florence would have no part in it; she didn't have time.

Florence's work during the Crimean War had been difficult on her physical health. By the early 1860s, she was seldom seen in public. Her condition often caused her to be confined to bed, although that didn't mean her efforts were forgotten. In 1907, she became the first woman to be awarded the Order of Merit for her work in nursing and public health. Florence Nightingale died on August 13, 1910, after laying a foundation on which the entire medical world would begin to build.

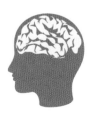

Words to Know

Morals: beliefs about what is good and bad behavior.

Convent: a Christian community of nuns.

Disciplined: well-trained in a certain skill and following strict rules that apply to it.

Administrative: relating to how a business or other organization is run. Administrative duties may include the tracking of how many products are sold, assigning employee time off, and managing money.

Efficiently: completed with as little waste as possible.

Public health: the branch of medicine focusing on ensuring an entire population is disease-free and physically and mentally sound.

Sanitation: public cleanliness. Sanitation programs provide clean water and proper waste disposal.

Feminist: a person, male or female, who supports equal rights for women.

Find Out More

Bostridge, Mark. *Florence Nightingale: The Making of an Icon*. New York: Farrar, Straus and Giroux, 2008.

Florence Nightingale
www.gale.cengage.com/free_resources/whm/bio/nightingale_f.htm.

Gill, Gillian. *Nightingales: The Extraordinary Upbringing and Curious Life of Miss Florence Nightingale*. New York: Random House, 2005.

Timko, Michael: "Florence Nightingale—Fantasy and Fact"
www.highbeam.com/doc/1G1-103614114.html.

6

Matilda Coxe Evans Stevenson:

Anthropologist of the American West

Anthropology is not a natural science like chemistry and biology; instead, it's considered to be a social science. When anthropology and other social sciences were getting started, women were often excluded, or they were treated as inferior scientists. One woman, however, Matilda Cox Evans Stevenson, earned recognition as an anthropologist.

Matilda Coxe Evans was born on May 12, 1849, in Texas. She didn't live there long, though; soon her family moved to Washington, D.C. Her father was a lawyer, writer, and journalist, and he made enough money to send his children to private schools. Matilda and her four brothers and sisters were first taught at home and then sent to boarding schools. Matilda went to Miss Anable's Academy in Philadelphia, where she received what was considered at the time to be an appropriate education for a young girl.

What Does Anthropology Mean?

Anthropology is the study of people. Cultural anthropologists study people's culture—that is, what people believe and how they live. Physical anthropologists study the biological evolution and variation of humans. Forensic anthropologists use physical anthropology to solve crimes.

In 1872, she married James Stevenson, who was a geologist and anthropologist. He worked for the U.S. Geological Survey, and he brought his wife along on several of his **expeditions** into the West. However, Matilda Evans Stevenson wasn't just a passenger, enjoying the sights. She wanted to work alongside her husband, and soon, she began to help him collect fossils. Their collections are still part of the Smithsonian Museum in Washington, D.C.

On one trip to the West, Matilda began studying Native American culture. First, she learned how to do anthropological studies from her husband. Then she applied her new knowledge to the study of the Ute and Arapaho Native Americans. Although she never published what she learned, it was a way for her to perfect her technique in anthropology.

Matilda's husband was eventually sent to New Mexico to study the Zuni people. He was working for the Bureau of American Ethnology, which collected information about Native Americans living in the western part of the country. Matilda worked as her husband's unpaid assistant. She and the rest of the group studied the Zuni for six months.

Most anthropologists at the time were men. Because they were men, they sometimes had a hard time studying women in the groups of people with which they were working. In fact, most male anthropologists didn't even bother thinking about the point of view of women they were studying! They only focused on the men in their studies.

Matilda helped to change that. While her husband collected data for the Bureau of American Ethnology, she made her own investigations. She studied the Zuni women and children, observing their roles and **rituals**. She ended up pub-

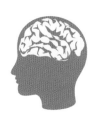

The United States Geological Survey

The U.S. government created the United States Geological Survey in 1879, to explore and document the western part of the United States. The country had recently added large amounts of land after the Louisiana Purchase and the Mexican-American War, and the government wanted to know what was out there. Today, the USGS studies the entire country. It focuses on topics like climate change, the health of ecosystems, water, and energy and mineral resources.

lishing a paper called "Religious Life of the Zuni Child," which was put out by the Bureau. She also published "The Zuni and the Zunians," which was meant for readers who weren't necessarily anthropologists.

After that trip, she continued to be part of many Bureau research teams, along with her husband. She was never paid for her work, however, despite her skill and hard work.

Several other female anthropologists were working around the same time as Matilda was. She understood the challenges they faced and organized them into the Women's Anthropological Society of America in 1885. She was the organization's first president. The society offered a place to support women's anthropological studies. At the time, women often had a hard time publishing papers or receiving money to conduct research.

Then, in 1888, James Stevenson died. Now, for the first time, the Bureau of American Ethnology hired Matilda, so that she could finish her husband's work. At first, it was only a temporary position so that she could complete the study they had started on the Zia Pueblo tribe. After that was done, however, she was hired for a permanent position. She was the first female anthropologist to be hired by the U.S. government.

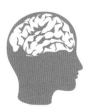

Matilda wrote: "It is my wish to erect a foundation upon which students may build... I think and hope it may open wide the gates for other students to pass the more rapidly over the many, many parts which I have left unexplored."

Matilda continued to work with the Zuni. She published more works about them, including *The Zuni Indians: Their Mythology, Esoteric Fraternities, and Ceremonies*. She wrote for many of the major scientific publications of the day, like *Science* and the *American Anthropologist*.

She eventually moved to New Mexico, to be closer to the people she had studied and lived with for so long. She continued to compile research until she died in 1915. Her work paved the way for other anthropologists, especially women.

Words to Know

Expeditions: journeys by groups of people with a particular research purpose.
Rituals: ceremonies with steps that are the same every time they are performed; rituals are often religious, but do not have to be.

Find Out More

Encyclopedia Britannica: "Matilda Coxe Evans Stevenson"
www.britannica.com/EBchecked/topic/565974/Matilda-Coxe-Stevenson

Thomas, Peggy. *Talking Bones: The Science of Forensic Anthropology*. New York: Facts on File, 2008.

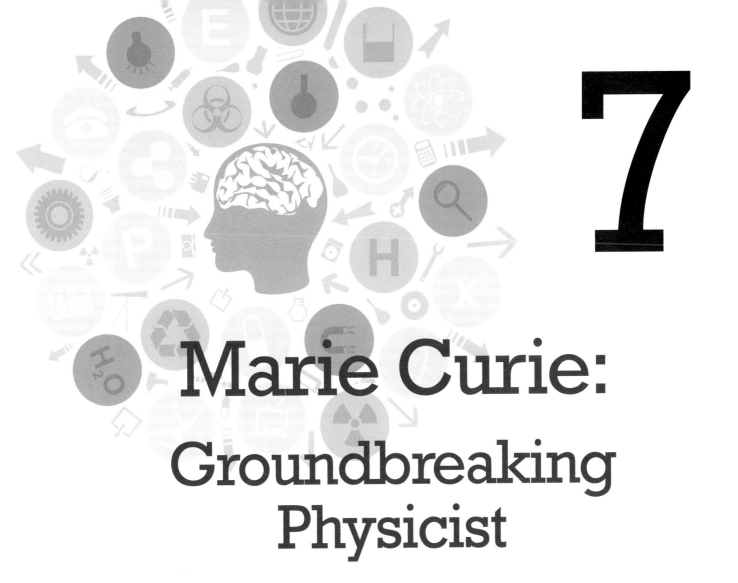

7

Marie Curie: Groundbreaking Physicist

Marie Curie is the best-known woman scientist, and one of the best-known of all scientists. She gave her life for her science. But she never knew that her scientific investigation was what killed her.

Marya Sklodowska was born November 7, 1867, in Warsaw, Poland. She was the youngest child of two educators. Her mother was a pianist and teacher. Her father was a mathematics and physics professor. After her mother died just before Marya's tenth birthday, she spent many hours with her father, eagerly learning about chemistry and physics.

She seemed to have an endless thirst for knowledge, and she was a quick learner. At school, Marya was at the top of her class and graduated from high school when she was only fifteen years old. After graduation from high school, though, there were few opportunities for women to obtain a higher education

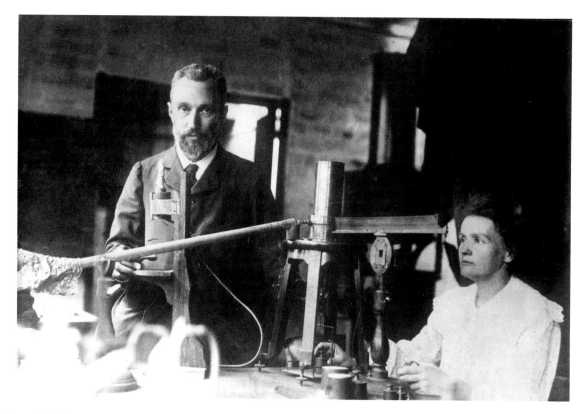

Marie with her husband Pierre in their lab. Marie was the first woman to ever win a Nobel Prize and the first person to win two Nobel Prizes.

in Poland. Marya's best opportunity for an advanced education was to attend the Sorbonne in Paris. Although supportive of Marya's desire for an advanced education, her family did not have the resources to send her to Paris. But Marya was not going to give up. She and her sister Bronya came up with a plan. Marya would work as a **governess** and tutor and use the money to help pay Bronya's medical school expenses. Once Bronya received her degree and became a doctor, she would help pay Marya's expenses at the Sorbonne.

So, for eight years, Marya worked hard as a tutor, earning and sending money to Bronya, who was studying at the Sorbonne. Marya continued to study on her own, and she participated in a program conducted by Polish professors. The program, taught to women **excluded** from the universities, was held in secret, because it was against the law.

In November 1891, Marya was finally able to leave Poland and enroll at the Sorbonne. She registered as "Marie," using the French spelling of her name. She

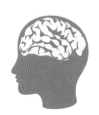

stayed with Bronya and her husband for a while, but eventually, she moved to an attic closer to the school. She did not want to waste time going back and forth to school, so she was willing to live in the almost **hovel**-like apartment. Marie lived **frugally**, but even so, she often did not have money for food. Her attic apartment was so cold at times that she could only sleep if all her clothing was piled on top of her for additional warmth. Marie was often ill from these conditions, but she continued to work hard and graduated at the top of her class with a degree in physics in 1893. In 1894, Marie received a master's degree in mathematics.

After graduation, Marie took a job doing research for an industrial society. She planned to work for a while but eventually return to Poland and teach. Instead, she met Pierre Curie, a professor in the School of Physics. They married in 1895.

Marie was interested in studying **radiation**. X-rays had been discovered in 1895, and in 1896 it was discovered that uranium emitted similar amounts of radiation as X-rays did. Using techniques Pierre developed, Marie studied uranium and other ore radiation. She discovered that there was a property in the uranium itself that affected the atom. Marie called this radioactivity. Pierre abandoned his own work to help with Marie's research.

Historical Background

In the late 1800s, Poland was divided into three parts by its neighbors Russia, Prussia, and Austria. Warsaw was located in the Russian part of Poland, and the Russians kept a tight control over the Polish people. Russian school inspectors made sure young children were being taught the approved curriculum. Marya and her sisters attended a school where the teachers taught the girls forbidden subjects such as sciences and Polish history and language, while reporting that they taught approved subjects like home economics. If an inspector appeared unexpectedly, the teachers and students switched subjects immediately until he had gone.

Their research led to the discovery of a stronger radioactive element in 1898, which the couple named polonium, after Poland. Later in 1898, they discovered an even more radioactive element: radium. They announced their discoveries on December 26, 1898, but it wasn't until 1902 that Marie was able to definitively prove the existence of radium.

Marie's ability to prove that radium existed brought her a doctorate—the first ever granted to a woman in Europe. It also brought Marie and Pierre the Nobel Prize in Physics in 1903. The Curies were international celebrities, and for the first time in their careers, they had enough money to support their research. The French government was so proud of the couple that it wanted to award Pierre a professorship in physics at the Sorbonne and provide Marie with a new laboratory. Sadly, Pierre was killed in an accident before they could accept the offer.

After Pierre's death, Marie did not give up. Instead, she accomplished another first. She assumed the professorship that the government had planned to give to Pierre, becoming the first female faculty member at the Sorbonne. She ran the Radium Institute at the Sorbonne as well as a laboratory in Warsaw, and her research brought her another Nobel Prize in 1911, this time in Chemistry.

When World War I broke out, Marie did not want to sit on the sidelines. She brought X-ray machines to the battlefield, which saved countless lives of wounded servicemen. Once the war was over, Marie worked tirelessly to raise funds to support the medical use of X-rays and radium. She also worked for world peace and became involved with the League of Nations.

By the end of the 1920s, Marie suffered from **chronic** fatigue and nausea. **Cataract** operations only partially restored her fading eyesight. An almost-constant humming interfered with her hearing. Research showed that many others who had worked closely with radium also suffered from similar conditions. Some had died at relatively young ages. Though Marie at first denied that radium could be the cause of the illnesses and deaths, she eventually had no choice but to accept the fact that radium could be dangerous. She refused to stop her research, though, and continued working despite her fragile health. Then, in the early 1930s, Marie developed **pernicious anemia**. Doctors determined that it was caused by her lengthy exposure to radium, but they withheld the information from her. Marie Curie died on July 4, 1934, at the age of sixty-six.

The importance of Marie Curie's contributions to science cannot be over-stated. She built foundations for the modern world and influenced countless men and women with her example.

Words to Know

Excluded: Left out, barred from entry.

Governess: a woman hired to raise and educate the children of a household.

Hovel: a small, miserable house or hut.

Frugally: using little money or material.

Radiation: a stream of particles transmitted from radioactive atoms and molecules as they decay.

Chronic: long-lasting, particularly an illness.

Cataract: an eye disease that makes the eye cloudy, resulting in blurry vision.

Pernicious anemia: a severe form of anemia caused by the stomach's inability to absorb vitamin B-12 and leading to a lack of red blood cells and oxygen deprivation in the body's internal organs.

Find Out More

Biography: "Marie Curie"
www.nobelprize.org/nobel_prizes/physics/laureates/
1903/marie-curie-bio.html

Curie, Eve. *Madame Curie: A Biography* (trans. by Vincent Sheean). New York: Da Capo, 2001.

Ogilvie, Marilyn Bailey. *Marie Curie: A Biography*. Westport, Conn.: Greenwood Press, 2004.

8

Ellen Swallow Richards
The First Ecologist

It's not often that a scientist invents a new kind of science. Ellen Swallow Richards did. She was one of the first people to use the word "**ecology**," and she dedicated her life to ecological research. Ecology means the study of the environment, and as a chemist, Ellen believed that ecology was the key to improving people's lives.

Ellen Swallow was born in 1842 in Dunstable, Massachusetts. Her family was fairly poor, and she didn't have any formal education until she was sixteen. However, Ellen was intelligent, and she ended up teaching school and tutoring. She knew she wanted to go to college, and so she saved up money from her teaching jobs and cleaning houses. Eventually, she made enough money and managed to get into Vassar College when she was twenty-six. She skipped her first two years, and entered as a third-year student.

Ellen especially liked her chemistry and astronomy classes at Vassar. Some of her professors influenced her later thinking. A chemistry professor named Charles Farrar convinced her it was important to think about science in the household. Science can be applied anywhere, even the home. Ellen also had an astronomy professor named Maria Mitchell, who worked hard to ensure women had a place in the sciences. She saw how intelligent and hardworking Ellen was, and she wanted her to continue with science.

Maria Mitchell

Maria Mitchell is considered the first female astronomer in the United States. Her father was also an astronomer, and he encouraged her to build on her natural talent for science. Early on, she was only the second woman ever to discover a comet. She went on to teach at Vassar College, where she taught potential female scientists such as Ellen Swallow Richards. Mitchell was the first woman to become a member of the American Academy of Arts and Sciences.

After graduating from Vassar, Ellen did continue with her chemistry studies. She applied to jobs, but all her applications were turned down. She knew she had to learn more if she hoped to be a chemist, so she applied to universities. Most turned her down, simply because she was a woman. One did accept her, though: the Massachusetts Institute of Technology (MIT). She was the only woman MIT accepted, because they wanted to see how a woman would do in the sciences. She was an experiment of sorts. Luckily, she proved that women could be excellent scientists, just like men.

While at MIT, Ellen earned the respect of her professors and fellow students. She studied water science, and quickly became an expert. At the end of her time studying at MIT, the other students in her lab gave her an honorary degree, called an A.O.M.: Artium Omnium Magistra, which is Latin for Mistress of All the

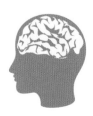

Arts. She studied at MIT for three years, and ended up with another bachelor's degree. She also received a master's from Vassar, because she sent her old school a **thesis** in chemistry.

She wasn't leaving MIT, though. She took a job as a lab assistant with the head of her chemistry laboratory at MIT. She also married a professor of mining, Robert Hallowell Richards. Her husband was very supportive of her continued scientific research.

While continuing her own research, Ellen wanted to help more women enter the sciences. She helped set up the Women's Laboratory at MIT in 1876. The lab offered a place for more women to do research and get an education. A few years later, she became an assistant instructor in the Women's Laboratory, although she wasn't paid for her work. While there, Ellen focused on science in the home. She looked at food safety, good nutrition and fitness, sanitation, and clothing. Men had overlooked these topics in the past, but Ellen was determined to make the home a safer and healthier place to live. The Women's Laboratory wasn't open for long. It closed less than ten years after it opened, because MIT began accepting women into regular classes and labs rather than keeping them together in a special laboratory.

Meanwhile, Ellen was moving up. In 1884, she was hired as an instructor at MIT and given a salary. She focused on what she called "sanitary chemistry" and continued to do research as well as teach. Her work started to have a big effect outside MIT too. In 1887, the Massachusetts government hired her for a project. She and her team researched the water quality in all the ponds and lakes in the state, to see how polluted they were. In the end, their findings led to some big changes. Massachusetts set up state water quality standards (the first in the country). The state also built a new sewage treatment plant, to decrease the amount of pollution that Ellen had found in the lakes and ponds of Massachusetts. The government was so impressed with her work that it appointed her as the official water analyst for the State Board of Health.

Ellen was very busy at this point in her life. She was working for the state and for MIT. She also found time to write books. She first wrote *The Chemistry of Cooking and Cleaning: A Manual for Housekeepers*. Later, she wrote another book with another scientist called *Air, Water, and Food from a Sanitary Standpoint*. She went on to publish seventeen books in all, including the first health food cookbook in the United States.

This image shows the laboratory where Ellen tested water samples. Ellen wrote, "Let Ecology be henceforth the science of [our] normal lives ... the worthiest of all the applied sciences which teaches the principles on which to found healthy and happy life."

That wasn't all she did. Ellen also worked as a chemist at the Manufacturer's Mutual Fire Insurance Company, set up the first school lunch programs in Boston, improved sanitation in schools, and created exhibits for world fairs. She also organized the Lake Placid Conference in Home Economics. Of course, she was the first president of the group. Ellen continued to work up until her death in 1911. Her intelligence, passion, and hard work made a lasting difference in the world. Other scientists, both men and women, have followed in her footsteps, building on the discoveries she made. Most of all, she helped the world understand the importance of ecology.

Words to Know

Ecology: the study of living things and their interactions with the environment.
Thesis: a long essay written to complete a doctoral program and receive a Master's degree or PhD.

Find Out More

Richards Swallow, Ellen. *The Chemistry of Cooking and Cleaning*. Charleston, S.C.: BiblioLife, 2009.

Vassar Encyclopedia: "Ellen Swallow Richards"
vcencyclopedia.vassar.edu/alumni/ellen-swallow-richards.html

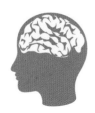

Elizabeth Lee Hazen & Rachel Fuller Brown:

Antifungal Inventors

9

oday, most people take **antibiotics** for granted. In fact, many experts believe that some members of the medical community use them too much, thereby making them less effective over time and creating a group of diseases resistant to antibiotics. There are, however, some people for whom a particular type of antibiotics—the **antifungals**—mean life or death. Without the work of Elizabeth Hazen and Rachel Fuller Brown these people would not be able to be alive.

Elizabeth Hazen was born in Rich, Mississippi, on August 24, 1885. When she was three years old, Elizabeth was orphaned, and she and her two siblings went to live with their maternal grandmother. Eventually, they moved in with their father's brother and his family, which included three children of his own.

Elizabeth attended a one-room school. After graduating from high school, she received private tutoring in Memphis, Tennessee, to improve her chances of success in college. She was accepted to Mississippi State College for Women (now Mississippi University for Women), where she earned a Bachelor of Science degree. For six years, Elizabeth taught at Central High School in Jackson, Mississippi. During the summer, she took classes at the University of Tennessee and the University of Virginia.

In 1905, Elizabeth moved to New York City to do graduate work at Columbia University. Many at Columbia doubted Elizabeth's likelihood of success in the **competitive** graduate program. Their doubts were not based so much on her gender as the fact that she had been educated in the South. At the time, many believed that the southern educational system was inferior to that of other parts of the country.

Elizabeth proved that she was capable of success. She obtained a master's degree in biology and then enrolled in the university's College of Physicians and Surgeons to study medical **bacteriology**. She put her education on hold during World War I, when she served in **diagnostic** labs in New York and Alabama.

Instead of returning to school after the war, Elizabeth accepted a position as the director of a hospital's clinical laboratory in West Virginia. She did return to the College of Physicians and Surgeons in 1923, where she completed a doctorate in **microbiology**. She went to work at Columbia Presbyterian Hospital and the College of Physicians and Surgeons.

In 1931, Elizabeth moved to the Division of Laboratories and Research of New York State's Department of Health, where she headed the Bacterial Diagnosis Laboratory in New York City. Augustus Wadsworth, head of the division, chose her in 1944 to lead research into fungi. She returned to Columbia's College of Physicians and Surgeons to study mycology, the branch of botany that specializes in the scientific study of fungi. By 1948, Elizabeth had discovered antifungal **agents** among bacteria.

At this point, Elizabeth had gone as far as she could. To look for specific substances with antifungal characteristics required a chemist. Rachel Fuller Brown was selected to head up that part of the research.

48 SCIENTIFIC FOUNDATIONS

Rachel Fuller Brown had been born in Springfield, Massachusetts, on November 23, 1898. She and her family moved to Webster Groves, Missouri, where she attended elementary school. When Rachel was twelve, her father, a real estate agent, left the family. Rachel, her mother, and younger brother moved back to Springfield, where her mother supported the family by working as a secretary and director of religious education for local churches.

Thanks to the support of a family friend and a small scholarship, after her high-school graduation Rachel was able to attend Mount Holyoke College in South Hadley, Massachusetts. She majored in history and chemistry. Rachel next taught at a private girls' school, and then, in 1924, went on to the University of Chicago to earn a doctorate in chemistry and bacteriology. She took a position with the New York Department of Health's Division of Laboratories and Research in Albany that interrupted her education, but eventually she did earn her doctorate.

In 1948, Elizabeth and Rachel began their work together. Though hundreds of miles apart, Elizabeth and Rachel **collaborated** on groundbreaking research on antibiotics to fight fungal infections. Conditions caused by fungal infections, such as certain central nervous system disorders, athlete's foot, and ringworm, had no cure at the time. Penicillin, invented in 1928, and similar antibiotics were the main treatment methods for infections, but among their potential side effects were fungal infections.

Elizabeth and Rachel searched for microorganisms that would produce antibiotics. Elizabeth collected soil samples from a friend's farm and found that they contained two fungus-fighting substances. She sent the samples to Rachel, who **isolated** the antifungal substances. One proved fatal in animals. The other, however, showed promise. It wasn't toxic to animals, and it fought candidiasis (a type of fungal infection that often affects the throat and respiratory tract), as well as a fungus that affected the lungs and central nervous system. In honor of the New York State Department of Health, the duo named the substance nystatin.

Their discovery was announced in 1950. The state had no resources for large-scale **clinical trials** or the ability to mass-produce nystatin, so **patent** rights were sold to pharmaceutical manufacturer E. R. Squibb. **Royalties** were contributed to the Brown-Hazen Research Fund, which provided grants to those researching the life sciences throughout the life of the patent.

This image shows Elizabeth and Rachel in a lab together in 1955, the year that they won the Squibb Award in Chemotherapy.

Nystatin proved to be effective in nonhuman conditions as well. It has been used in the treatment of Dutch elm disease and has also been used to combat the development of mold in water-damaged artworks.

In 1955, Elizabeth and Rachel received the Squibb Award in Chemotherapy. In 1975, they became the first women to receive the Chemical Pioneer Award from the American Institute of Chemists.

Elizabeth continued working in antifungal research for another decade. She returned to Columbia as **professor emeritus** and was a consultant for the Division of Laboratories and Research. She died on June 24, 1975.

After her co-discovery, Rachel was promoted to biochemist in 1951. On her retirement in 1968, she received the Distinguished Service Award from the New York State Department of Health. In 1972, the Medical Mycological Society of the Americas awarded her the Rhoda Benham Award. Rachel died on January 14, 1980.

Both Rachel and Elizabeth were important scientists. Together, they created the foundations on which future work could be built.

Words to Know

Antibiotics: substances, usually produced by or developed from microorganisms, that destroy or prohibit the growth of other microorganisms.

Antifungals: medicines used to get rid of tiny living things called fungi that have invaded the body.

Competitive: wanting to be better than others, or wanting to win.

Bacteriology: the study of tiny, one-celled organisms that often cause disease, called bacteria.

Diagnostic: related to the process of identifying illness and disease in medical patients.

Microbiology: the study of tiny living things that can only be seen with a microscope, such as fungi and bacteria.

Agents: people or things that produce a specific effect.

Collaborated: worked together on.

Isolated: identified and obtained in a pure form.

Clinical trials: controlled tests of new drugs using human beings as subjects.

Patent: the right to make, use, or sell an invention, usually given by a government to the inventor for a specific amount of time.

Royalties: money given to an inventor for using his or her invention; royalties may also be given to authors, musicians, and others based on how many works have been sold or used.

Professor emeritus: a title given to a retired professor.

Find Out More

Camp, Carole Ann. *American Women Inventors*. Berkeley Heights, N.J.: Enslow, 2004.

Haven, Kendall F. *Women at the Edge of Discovery: 40 True Science Adventures*. Westport, Conn.: Libraries Unlimited, 2003.

Inventor of the Week: "Elizabeth Lee Hazen and Rachel Fuller Brown" web.mit.edu/invention/iow/HazenBrown.html

Waisman, Charlotte, and Jill Titejen. *Her Story: A Timeline of Women Who Changed America*. New York: Collins, 2008.

10

Elizabeth Donnell Kay:

Environmentalist

Many scientists appreciate the visible natural world. Geologists study rocks, water, and landforms. Botanists study plants. Zoologists study animals. Environmentalists study both and the interactions between plants, animals, and their surrounding world. Elizabeth Donnell Kay is one scientist who studied the natural world, especially plants.

Elizabeth Donnell Kay was born in 1894. She was an only child. Her father was an Irish immigrant, an important business figure in Philadelphia. Her mother was from a well-known Philadelphia family. Together, her parents could give Elizabeth a good education. She attended the Master's School in Dobbs Ferry, New York.

The Garden Club of America

The Garden Club of America was started in 1913. The goal of the club early on was to record the history of gardens in the United States. Today, the club's goals are "to promote greater understanding of the interdependence of horticulture, environmental protection, and community improvement." It hosts conferences, awards scholarships and funding, and leads educational programs. There are about 18,000 members nationwide.

In 1915, she married Alfred G. Kay, a stockbroker, and then moved to New Jersey. They had enough money to spend winters in Florida, while living in New Jersey the rest of the year. Elizabeth was generous with her money. She and her husband were very active in their Florida community, and they donated money to many worthy causes. They set up a hospital, a school, and a **civic association**.

Although she had a wide variety of interests, Elizabeth was particularly interested in the environment. She studied plants, animals, and ecosystems, and she was soon working to promote **conservation**. She started an herbal mail-order business in 1924. Teaching was always important to her as well; she often taught others about protecting native species of plants, and she taught farmers alternatives to burning their fields after harvesting (which cleared the fields, but also killed many living things).

Elizabeth also supported scientific research. She founded a research center in Florida that was dedicated to tropical plants. Researchers could bring in species of tropical plants to the center to test whether they could be grown in a southern Florida climate. Elizabeth wrote about horticulture and ecology, and she edited a book called *The Plant World in Florida*. She was also a president of the Garden Club of America.

Perhaps Elizabeth's greatest contribution to her Florida home was the Pine Jog Environmental Education Center. She and her husband donated land and money to set up the southern Florida center. They had bought Pine Jog Plantation a few years before, and they wanted to open it to the public as a way to

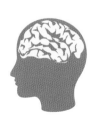

educate others about the environment. It is still in operation, and today tens of thousands of people visit the center every year.

Elizabeth's **legacy** also includes another environmental education center in New Jersey. She and her husband gave their New Jersey property to the public. The county Park Commission turned the land into the Elizabeth D. Kay Environmental Education Center. Visitors can learn about the local landscape, and enjoy hiking through a variety of ecosystems. Like the other women in this book, Elizabeth proved that women can understand science—and that by doing so, they can help build a better world.

Words to Know

Civic association: a group of people who try to improve a neighborhood through volunteer work.

Conservation: the protection and restoration of the natural environment, including habitats, animals, or plants.

Legacy: something passed on to future generations.

Find Out More

Historical Society of Chester, New Jersey: "Elizabeth Donnell Kay"
www.historicchesternj.com/peopleplaces/miscellaneouspeople.html

Kessler, Colleen. *Hands-On Ecology*. Waco, Tex.: Prufrock, 2006.

Pine Jog Environmental Education Center
www.pinejog.fau.edu

Opportunities for Women Today in Science

In the past, women were rejected from universities, given little or no pay for their work, and were often not recognized for the groundbreaking research they did. Times have changed a lot for women in science today. Although challenges are left for women scientists to overcome, women now have a proper place in the world of science. Women are science students, professors, researchers, and leaders. The opportunities for women in science are always expanding.

Science Studies

Recently there has been a big push toward getting girls and women interested in the sciences. People have realized that in order to advance in science, we need to include everyone. If we have women working in science, we'll be able to create more research questions, solve more problems, and make the world a better place.

Today, girls study science in about the same number as boys. In college, the numbers of men and women getting bachelor's degrees in science are about the same as well. Over 45 percent of recent science and engineering bachelor's degree recipients were women. By comparison, only 23 percent of science and engineering graduates over sixty-five are women.

The story is a little different as students enter graduate school. The number of women who get PhDs in science is fewer than men. In 2009, only 33 percent of PhD graduates in physical and earth sciences were women. Twenty-seven percent of graduates in computer science were women. Things are a little different in the biological sciences, where 51 percent of graduates were women. And in the social sciences, 60 percent of PhD graduates were women.

The way is open for women who want to study science. Larger numbers of women are studying science in college, and some are continuing on to get their PhDs. We've come a long way from the days when women were forbidden from studying science!

Jobs

All types of science jobs are open to women these days. They can be college professors, run research labs, or work for businesses. It's no longer unusual to see a woman in any of these settings.

Science can offer a promising career to many people, men and women alike. Here are some job growth forecasts for different kinds of scientists, between 2010 and 2020:

- Atmospheric scientists: 11 percent growth, driven by industry
- Biochemists and biophysicists: 31 percent growth, driven by the need for new drugs and cleaner energy

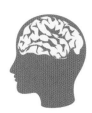

- Environmental scientists: 19 percent growth, driven by increased interest in the environment, and more environmental regulations
- Geoscientists: 21 percent growth, driven by the need for better land management
- Microbiologists: 13 percent growth, driven by the need for new drugs
- Physicists and astronomers: 14 percent growth, driven by more government spending on research
- Psychologists: 22 percent growth, driven by more hiring by schools, hospitals, and social service agencies

There will be thousands of new jobs in these areas of science and others. Women graduating with science degrees can look forward to many opportunities, no matter their field.

Women will have thousands of career opportunities in science during the twenty-first century. One of these jobs might be right for you!

These two science students may be equally intelligent and committed to their work—but the female student is likely to face challenges that her male peer won't. However, women have proven for centuries that they can overcome challenges!

A Long Way to Go

Although more and more women are becoming scientists, not everything is equal yet. Some fields of science, especially the physical sciences like geology and physics, are still male dominated. Although equal numbers of men and women study science in college, fewer women go on to get jobs in their field. People have been researching why for many years.

One reason is that women often feel the need to choose between having a career and having a family. Some researchers have found that there are about the same number of single men and women scientists. However, there are fewer married women than married men, and even fewer women with children than men with children. That's because the sciences are not always the easiest place for a woman to balance having a family and a career. Science careers often demand long hours. The United States also doesn't provide much support for mothers (or fathers) who need to take time off from their jobs to have children. In other countries, parents are allowed to leave their jobs for a few months to take care of young children. Their jobs are secure while they take time off, and when they come back to work, day-care is available. Women who take too much time off

for family reasons in the United States might lose their jobs. Some women simply leave science while they raise families. Most fathers, however, keep working, because in our country, some people still think that women should be the ones to take care of children.

Some people think that women still face **prejudice** in science too. One recent study backs up that idea. The report found that science professors were more likely to give male science studens better opportunities than female science students.

Researchers asked a group of science professors to take a look at a job application a "student" had made for a lab manager position. The application was made up, but the professors thought it was real. Half the applications had the name John on them, and the other half had the name Jennifer. Otherwise, they were exactly the same. The researchers found that both male and female professors were less favorable to the female applicant, even though the application was exactly the same as the male applicant's. They were less likely to offer her the job, and when they did, they offered her a lower salary.

The report showed that there is still a hidden **bias** against women in the sciences. Probably none of those professors in the study would have said they were **sexist**, but their actions show that they still considered men more qualified as scientists.

Women today still have challenges to face, such as lower pay and gender bias, before they can truly be equal in the sciences. But the female scientists of the past built the foundation on which today's women can build. Those courageous women broke down barriers. They laid the groundwork for today's women. Because of them, little girls growing up today can be engineers and astronomers, doctors and biologists, physicists and inventors. In fact, they can be anything they want to be!

Words to Know

Prejudice: an opinion, usually negative, about someone not based on experience or facts. Prejudice often involves dislike or distrust of an ethnicity, religion, gender, or another minority group.

Bias: an unfair preference for or against someone or something, which leads to unfair treatment.

Sexist: an attitude of believing one gender is better than another, which can lead to discrimination.

Find Out More

Gornick, Vivian. *Women in Science: Then and Now*. New York: The Feminist Press, 2009.

Purcell, Karen. *Unlocking Your Brilliance: Smart Strategies for Women to Thrive in Science, Technology, Engineering, and Math*. Austin, Tex.: Greenleaf Book Group, 2012.

Thimmesh, Catherine. *Girls Think of Everything: Stories of Ingenious Inventions by Women*. Torrance, Calif.: Sandpiper, 2002.

U.S. Bureau of Labor Statistics: "Occupational Outlook Handbook: Life, Physical, and Social Sciences"
www.bls.gov/ooh/life-physical-and-social-science/home.htm

Index

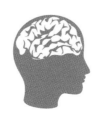

About the Author & Consultant

Kim Etingoff lives in Boston, Massachusetts, spending part of her time working on farms. Kim has written a number of books for young people on topics including health, history, nutrition, and business.

Ann Lee-Karlon, PhD, is the President of the Association for Women in Science (AWIS) in 2014–2016. AWIS is a national nonprofit organization dedicated to advancing women in science, technology, engineering, and mathematics. Dr. Lee-Karlon also serves as Senior Vice President at Genentech, a major biotechnology company focused on discovering and developing medicines for serious diseases such as cancer. Dr. Lee-Karlon holds a BS in Bioengineering from the University of California at Berkeley, an MBA from Stanford University, and a PhD in Bioengineering from the University of California at San Diego, where she was a National Science Foundation Graduate Research Fellow. She completed a postdoctoral fellowship at the University College London as an NSF International Research Fellow. Dr. Lee-Karlon holds several U.S. and international patents in vascular and tissue engineering.

Picture Credits

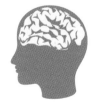

64